LITTLE LAMB
BAKES A CAKE

by Michaela Muntean · pictures by Nicole Rubel

COLLINS

Little Lamb wanted to make a
birthday cake for her mother,
and she wanted it to be a surprise.
But where do you begin when you
want to make a cake?

"I believe you begin with a recipe,"
said Little Lamb, so she looked in
the cookbook and found a recipe
for yellow cake.

Find the card with the picture of the cookbook.
Put it on the box with the number **1**.

Little Lamb read the recipe.
Then she looked in the refrigerator
and the cupboards.
There was a little bit of everything
but not enough of anything to make a cake.
So Little Lamb made a list of what
she needed.

Find the card with the picture of the shopping list.
Put it on the box with the number **2**.

Little Lamb took her list to the grocery store and rolled the metal cart up and down the aisles.

Flour, baking powder, milk, eggs, butter— soon she had the ingredients she needed to make a cake.

Find the card with the picture of the ingredients. Put it on the box with the number **3**.

When she got home, Little Lamb took the groceries out of the basket and set them on the counter.

"Oh dear!" she cried. "I forgot to buy sugar, and without sugar my cake will not be sweet."

So Little Lamb went next door and borrowed a cup of sugar from Black Sheep.

Find the card with the picture of the cup of sugar.
Put it on the box with the number **4**.

"*Now* I have everything I need to make a cake," said Little Lamb, and she put on her apron and set to work.

She mixed the butter and sugar together in a big mixing bowl.

Find the card with the picture of the mixing bowl.
Put it on the box with the number **5**.

Then she cracked three eggs into a
little bowl and beat them with
an egg whisk.

Little Lamb felt very proud of herself.
Everything was going just as planned,
except that she had spilled a little
sugar and dropped an egg on the floor.

"I will clean up everything when I am
done making my cake," said Little Lamb.

Find the card with the picture of the egg whisk.
Put it on the box with the number **6**.

Little Lamb measured the flour in
a measuring cup.
She measured the baking powder with
a measuring spoon.
Then she sifted them in a bowl.

Find the card with the picture of the measuring cup,
measuring spoons, and sifter.
Put it on the box with the number **7**.

Quickly Little Lamb mixed all the
ingredients together in the biggest bowl she
could find, spilling just a little bit
of everything.

Then Little Lamb greased and floured
two round cake tins.
Very carefully she poured the mixture
into the tins.

Find the card with the picture of the cake tins.
Put it on the box with the number **8**.

"Now my cake is ready to bake,"
said Little Lamb.
She put the tins in the oven
and waited until the cake had baked
to a golden-brown colour.

While the cake was cooling on a rack,
Little Lamb made pink frosting.

Find the card with the picture of the oven.
Put it on the box with the number **9**.

She frosted the layers, and on the top of the cake Little Lamb made four yellow flowers.

Oh, Little Lamb's mother was going to be very, very surprised!

Now turn all the cards over, one by one, to make a surprise picture.